*To all the people who have
kept Africa's true histories
alive, even when it seemed
that so many were unwilling
to listen. Thank you.
–P.L.*

*To Mom and Dad
–J.G.*

The illustrations in this book were created digitally.
Set in Above the Sky, Recoleta, and Cabin.

Library of Congress Control Number 2021951830
ISBN 978-1-4197-6022-8

Text © 2022 Patrice Lawrence
Illustrations © 2022 Jeanetta Gonzales
Cover © 2022 Magic Cat
Book design by Zoë Tucker

Printed and bound in China
10 9 8 7 6 5 4 3 2 1

MIX
Paper from
responsible sources
FSC® C104723

FSC
www.fsc.org

ABRAMS The Art of Books
195 Broadway, New York, NY 10007
abramsbooks.com

written by
PATRICE LAWRENCE

illustrated by
JEANETTA GONZALES

OUR STORY Starts IN AFRICA

MAGIC CAT PUBLISHING

NEW YORK

Paloma is so excited. She is visiting her family in Trinidad. She loves feeling the warm Caribbean sun on her face and drinking fresh coconut water for breakfast while watching pale geckos scurry along Tante Janet's walls.

She wants to play with her cousins, but . . .

Her cousins don't want to play with her.
"You don't talk like us," they say.
"How can you be family?"

"Don't mind them," Tante Janet says.
"I'm going to tell you a secret."

Paloma loves secrets!

"You, me, and your cousins are from the oldest family
in the world," Tante Janet says. "And our story starts in Africa."

"My story doesn't start there, Tante!" Paloma says. "I wasn't born in Africa."

Tante smiles. "You see that comb you're holding? Archaeologists found combs like ours on the banks of the Nile River, in northeastern Africa. People like us were there thousands of years ago."

Why would a comb make me **African**? Paloma thinks.

Tante plucks the comb from Paloma's hand. "Maybe one of Africa's warrior queens tidied her hair with a comb like this after chasing invaders off her lands."

"Warrior queens?"

"Queen Amanirenas was fighting Romans two thousand years ago," Tante Janet says. "She was a ruler in the kingdom of Kush."

Paloma likes this part of the story! But why doesn't she know about Queen Amanirenas? "Did everyone forget her?" Paloma asks.

"No," Tante Janet says. "We African people have always told our stories.

We **wrote** them on parchment and carved them in stone.

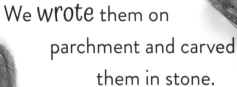

We **painted** them in caves and on jars.

We **tell** them in the weave of our kente cloth

and in the **beats** of our talking drums.

But best of all, we pass stories between each other, across thousands of years."

"Just like we're doing now, Tante!"

Paloma knows there's another way to save stories.
"Why didn't they just write books?" she asks.

"We did!" Tante replies.
"The Library of Alexandria had so many scrolls that
people traveled for miles and miles to study them."

"Mama takes me to the library every Wednesday," Paloma says. "Maybe we can go to Alexandria instead."

Tante Janet laughs sadly. "It's long gone, sweetness. But come, I'm thirsty after all this talking. I'll make some ginger beer."

Ginger beer! Paloma loves the way it makes her tongue tingle.

"First we need limes," Tante Janet says,
"to freshen the taste."

Tante's yard is full of trees that Paloma has never seen
before. "What's that one, Tante?" she asks.

"That's cocoa, Paloma. The pods are like treasure chests. The seeds inside are turned into chocolate."

"Africa is a treasure chest, too," Tante Janet says.
"Full of fruit and spice and precious wood like ebony.
For thousands of years, traders sailed across
the Red Sea to buy frankincense resin
to make perfume.

Some of the African rulers became very rich and built mighty kingdoms."

"But what about real treasure?"
Paloma asks. "Like gold and diamonds?"

"Oh yes!" Tante Janet says. "There was so much
of it that rulers from other countries
became jealous."

"They came to steal our
precious things,

including our most precious thing of all ..."

"...our people."

"That's how we came to Trinidad," Tante Janet says. "We were **stolen** from Africa and forced by rulers from Europe to work as slaves growing cocoa and sugar."

"Didn't our warrior queens fight back?" Paloma asks.

"They tried," Tante Janet says. "Our kings fought, too! It took hundreds of years to end slavery. But the rulers found another way to steal Africa's treasure.

They cut Africa into chunks.

Our lands were **chopped** up,

mixed up, and **squashed together**."

"The people who lived there had no say at all.
Our countries' names were changed—our languages, too."

"Don't you like speaking English, Tante?"

"Yes," Tante says. "But before
we were stolen, we spoke many
beautiful languages."

"What happened next, Tante?"

"One by one, the new countries freed
themselves from the European rulers,
though they could never return to how
they were before. Some took new
names and people had to learn
to live together."

"They're like cousins that don't
know each other."

"Just so," Tante Janet says.

Outside, the dark sky is now sprinkled with stars.

"I want to be an astronaut," Paloma says.

Tante Janet smiles. "Scientists have built a mighty new space telescope in South Africa. I'd travel all the way there to look through it and see you in your spaceship."

"I'll wave at you, Tante. And at my cousins, too. And when I pass over Africa, I'll wave at everyone there, because we're all family . . ."

"And our story starts in Africa!"

Dear Reader,

I was born in England but my mother was born in Trinidad, a small Caribbean island near the northern coast of South America. The first time I visited my family in Trinidad, I was six years old. I loved the beautiful island, but it was strange for me, because even though my cousins and I spoke English, we often couldn't understand each other because our accents were so different. As a child, I felt that I didn't belong in England because I was Black and nearly everyone else was white, but I didn't belong in Trinidad either because I didn't sound like everyone there!

As I grew older, I learned about the terrible history of people who had been kidnapped in Africa and forced to work on Caribbean plantations owned by white people. (A plantation was like a very big farm where crops like sugar and cocoa were grown to sell in Europe.) When I watched the news on TV, I also learned that countries in Africa were always at war or people were dying because there wasn't enough food or water. It wasn't until I was an adult that I learned about ancient Africa's rich history, its warrior queens, and how Africa was also full of many wonderful things that have shaped the rest of the world.

I hope you enjoyed celebrating the history of Africa with Paloma and Tante Janet. You may already know pieces of the story or none of it at all, but now I hope you want to find out even more. After all, Africa is made up of over fifty countries and all of those countries have their own stories, too. And you know what we should do with stories, don't you? Pass them on!

Love,
Patrice

Patrice Lawrence

Patrice Lawrence, MBE, is an award-winning writer.
Her debut YA novel, *Orangeboy*, won the
YA Book Prize and the Waterstones Children's Book Prize
for Older Fiction, along with being shortlisted
for the Costa Children's Book Award.
Patrice was born in Brighton, England, raised in
an Italian-Trinidadian family in mid-Sussex,
and now lives on England's South Coast.

Jeanetta Gonzales

Jeanetta Gonzales is a Los Angeles–based designer
and illustrator. She draws inspiration from nature,
capturing moods and moments evoking happiness,
positivity, and beauty. While illustrating this book, she
referenced her African heritage and history, and wanted
to show her fondness of lush, tropical environments
and bold color through her use of paint and digital
illustration. This is her first book for children.

Paloma's Questions

Paloma learns that her story starts in Africa,
but there's still more she wants to know!

Does everyone's story start in Africa?

Africa is sometimes called "the Cradle of Humankind." This means that scientists believe the first ever humans lived there thousands and thousands of years ago. Some of those people travelled away from Africa to different parts of the world, starting their stories elsewhere. Their bodies, including the color of their skin, changed to fit in with their new homes. So, while not all of us are African, us humans all came from Africa first!

What is an empire?

An empire is when rulers of one land take control of lands that belong to other people. For example, many countries in Europe became empires by taking control of lands in Africa and South America. It meant that those lands and everything in them "belonged" to the countries in Europe.

What is slavery?

A person is enslaved when they are forced to work for another person for free. People have taken other people as slaves for thousands of years, often during wars. For more than three hundred years, millions of African people were kidnapped and enslaved by Europeans to work on their plantations in the Caribbean and North, Central, and South America. This was called the transatlantic slave trade and was especially cruel. Many African people died on the sea journey as well as on the plantations.

What is Africa famous for now?

Africa is home to many different people, languages, and cultures. Without African music, there would be no Brazilian samba . . . and no rhythm and blues! There are many famous African sports stars, including Derartu Tulu from Ethiopia, who was the first Black African woman to win an Olympic gold medal; and Siya Kolisi, the first Black man to captain the South African rugby union team. And African environmentalists, like Wangari Muta Maathai from Kenya, have made our world a better place.

Why was Africa cut up into new countries?

For thousands of years, there were many different kingdoms in Africa and some of the rulers were very rich. Mansa Musa was a ruler of the Mali Empire in west Africa. He was thought to be the richest man in the world! But even when slavery became against the law, the rulers in European countries still wanted Africa's gold, cocoa, and other precious things. They didn't want to fight each other for the riches, so they decided to cut Africa into new countries and share those countries between them. This was called the Scramble for Africa. The African people who already lived on those lands fought back and were often treated harshly.

Do you want to read some more?

- *Africa, Amazing Africa: Country by Country*
  by Atinuke and illustrated by Mouni Feddag

- *The Ga Picture Alphabet*
  by Nii Ayikwei Parkes and illustrated by Avril Filomeno

- *Room for Everyone*
  by Naaz Khan and illustrated by Mercè López

- *Secrets of the Afro Comb: 6,000 Years of Art and Culture*
  by K. N. Chimbiri